Joone

Written &
Illustrated by

emily kate moon

DIAL BOOKS FOR YOUNG READERS · AN IMPRINT OF PENGUIN GROUP (USA) INC.

I dedicate this book to you, my young reader—happy and free!

♡ Emily

Dial Books For Young Readers
A division of Penguin Young Readers Group
Published by the Penguin Group | Penguin Group (USA) Inc., 375 Hudson Street, New York, New York 10014, U.S.A.
Penguin Group (Canada), 90 Eglinton Avenue East, Suite 700, Toronto, Ontario, Canada M4P 2Y3 (a division of Pearson Penguin Canada Inc.) | Penguin Books Ltd, 80 Strand, London WC2R 0RL,
England | Penguin Ireland, 25 St Stephen's Green, Dublin 2, Ireland (a division of Penguin Books Ltd) | Penguin Group (Australia), 707 Collins Street, Melbourne, Victoria 3008, Australia (a division
of Pearson Australia Group Pty Ltd) | Penguin Books India Pvt Ltd, 11 Community Centre, Panchsheel Park, New Delhi – 110 017, India | Penguin Group (NZ), 67 Apollo Drive, Rosedale, Auckland 0632,
New Zealand (a division of Pearson New Zealand Ltd) | Penguin Books, Rosebank Office Park, 181 Jan Smuts Avenue, Parktown North 2193, South Africa | Penguin China, B7 Jiaming Center, 27 East
Third Ring Road North, Chaoyang District, Beijing 100020, China | Penguin Books Ltd, Registered Offices: 80 Strand, London WC2R 0RL, England

Designed by Jennifer Kelly
Text set in Kingthings Clarity
Manufactured in China on acid-free paper

1 3 5 7 9 10 8 6 4 2

Library of Congress Cataloging-in-Publication Data | Moon, Emily Kate.
Joone / by Emily Kate Moon.   p. cm.
Summary: Five-year-old Joone, who likes ice cream sandwiches and the colors orange and purple, lives in a yurt with her grandfather and pet turtle, Dr. Chin.
ISBN 978-0-8037-3744-0 (hardcover) [1. Grandfathers–Fiction.] I. Title.   PZ7.M773Jo 2013   [E]—dc23   2012017536

The illustrations for this book were rendered in gouache and pencil on Strathmore drawing paper.

Special thanks to Jennifer, who believed in Joone first. And to Nancy, who saw what Joone could become.

My name is Joone.

Some people spell it with a U.
I spell it with a smiley face.

I'm five. But I can count to a hundred.

I like orange and purple and
ice-cream sandwiches.

And I only wear my orange dress.

That's Grandpa.
He can count to a thousand.

He used to be a scientist.
Now he's just my grandpa.

Every day Grandpa teaches me
something new.

He says every day I teach him
something new, too.

Yesterday I taught him how to
make a daisy crown.

Grandpa says it's important to do things for other people.

So, today, I'm organizing his books in rainbow order,

leaving an ice-cream sandwich in the mailbox for the mail lady,

and collecting rocks for Dr. Chin to climb.

Dr. Chin is my turtle.

I got him last year
when I was little.

Dr. Chin lives with me and Grandpa in our yurt.

Most houses are square, but a yurt is round.
Ours has nine windows and a skylight at the top.

Grandpa built it when he wasn't old.
Now he just fixes it.

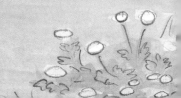

Sometimes Dr. Chin
and I help.

Sometimes we don't.

Then Grandpa says, "Joone! That dress is filthy!

You're not allowed to wear it till it's clean."

Good thing Dr. Chin loves swimming.

Dr. Chin and I are
always busy.

When Grandpa sees all our work, he says, "Joone,
I don't know where you find the energy."

And I say, "Grandpa, I don't know either!"

When Grandpa looks a little tired, I say, "Grandpa,
let's call it a day."

And he says, "That's a good idea, Joone."

Then, we all eat dinner together.

If I'm good, I get dessert.

At bedtime, Grandpa tucks me into bed,
and I read him a story.

If he's good, I read him two.

Then, I say, "Sleep well, Grandpa.
We have lots to do tomorrow!"

And he says, "Have sweet dreams, Joone."

So I do.